THE NEW BIZARRO AUTHOR SERIES

PRESENTS

I0629325

Nicholaus Patnaude

Eraserhead Press
Portland, OR

ERASERHEAD PRESS
P.O. BOX 10065
PORTLAND, OR 97296

WWW.ERASERHEADPRESS.COM

ISBN: 978-1-62105-232-6

Acknowledgments

I would like to thank my wife Sarah, my family, my son Rainer, my friends, my editor Garrett Cook, Eraserhead Press, Rose O'Keefe, Carlton Mellick III, and all the other folks in the thriving bizarro and underground literature communities who are producing so much inspiring and original work! Let's keep divergent thinking alive!

Foreword by Garrett Cook

Bizarro Fiction represents a giant spectrum of weirdness. There's stuff that's kinda weird, there's stuff that's genre with weird trappings, there's high parody, low parody and Saturday morning cartoon insanity. Then there's the kind of Bizarro Nicholaus Patnaude creates. Nick is the hard stuff. He's weird as fuck and doesn't need your permission. And that's what I like to see. It takes a lot to get that reaction out of me.

Guitar Wolf is ten thousand words of pure acidrock madness, the story of a band of animal instruments who ain't gonna take it anymore. The book is lean and mean, operating on a dream logic all its own while still having characters you can relate to. And it comes with three bonus stories that are equally off-the-wall and fun. Exciting stuff is about to happen for you. Nick is one of four authors handpicked this year to give you a glimpse of the genre's future and to introduce you to new writers in the Bizarro community. If you like this, lend the author your support with a review, a post on social media, or just by telling a friend. Enjoy the book!

Chapter One

The squealing feedback rang in Reggie's pointy, lupine ears. Trevor, lead guitarist of noise band 2666, riffed wildly over the poor wolf's aching midsection. Trevor had stitched and wired electric guitar pickups onto Reggie's belly. Bolts of electricity writhed like snakes in his bowels.

Trevor shotgunned a can of Bud Light, dripping fuzzy suds down his six-pack and treasure trail. Sticky globs of foam fell from his leather motorcycle jacket between the steel strings nailed and stapled from Reggie's forehead to his ass. Reggie: the wolf guitar. A noise band playing living animal instruments usually drew at least a modest crowd to the gigs.

A tan blonde in a neon pink bikini flipped up the visor of her helmet. Her rubber wolf mask seemed to leer. "Trevor, you put me in a trance. Can I climb up and hang out in the stars with you sometime? I love how your wicked dreams take me away. Far away."

Trevor blushed. They continued to flirt.

Denny's face pinched inward with a bluish hue. He looked like a rice farmer the way the cymbal was strapped to his head. The bruises to his turtle skin darkened after the 3 hours of inspired pounding by drummer Daryl during the final, recently concluded show of 2666's 3-night residency at The Burning Palladium. Tied by his wrists and legs to a bicycle wheel, Denny's chipped shell also bore traces of the decadent ecstasy of 2666's innumerable noise concerts.

Grace, (or: Alligator Girl as she'd been known in the freakshow), shook off a series of fuzz-box pedals out of the

7

input plugs scattered over her body like extra nipples. "You guys ever feel like you're being lightly electrocuted even hours after a show?"

Denny grimaced.

A drop of blood fell from her scaly, green snout as Grace stood on her hind legs. Her hands were firmly tied behind her back with rope and her neck was wrapped in a collar of barbwire. A series of synthesizer keys jutted from her reptilian armpits and sides. Her body shook as she sobbed.

"Remember when they killed the turtle in Cannibal Holocaust? Haha. That was the funniest scene." Jed, the sinewy curly-haired synth player chuckled into his Iphone 6 as he lay amidst chords and plugs on the wooden stage. He cracked a Bud Light and sipped it gingerly. "What did you just say? They eat live monkey brains in Faces of Death? Did somebody check it out yet from Lurchzillas?"

Reggie the wolf guitar arched his back like he didn't care if it broke in two. He bared his fangs and arched and stretched until spots and pain and muscle breakage told him to stop. Saliva streamed down his chin. Sweat poured down his furry sides. First one. Then two. The guitar strings of his imprisonment were finally breaking.

Ruffles, the Theremin gold-ax playing Golden Retriever—and the only living animal instrument of 2666 who participated willingly—had probably o.d.'d again. He lay with his tongue hanging out beside his golden ax (Max). Reggie picked up the weapon, gripped it in his clawed paws, raised it above his head, and roared like an angry god.

Chapter Two

Grace
2 Years ago

Grace wore a blue, silk robe. She trembled, dreading what Jed would say next.

The log cabin's floor-to-ceiling window overlooked a rushing river within the exhaust-like haze of the Blue Ridge Mountains.

"Please, Grace. This painting will be for the cover of our first album. We're thinking of calling it X-Rated Everglade. The first moment I saw you at the carnival, Gracie, I knew two things. One: I needed to save you. Two: I needed to paint you." Jed licked his lips and kneeled at Grace's reptile-skinned human feet.

The robe fell to the floor like a handful of dead butterflies. Her feet were frog green, exuding red thorns. A sheen of sweat on her scaly legs shimmered in the sunset light. Curly black hairs covered her lower stomach and pubis. Her upper chest narrowed inward like the sternum of an alligator. Although her nipples were thick and pronounced, her skin there was yellow, plated, and devoid of breasts.

Jed's smile could only mean one thing: he was an artist in love with his subject. All the gawkers and hecklers, drunk and dusty on the midway, were liars and thieves and psychopaths. She would give Jed everything. Her life. Her love. Her entire being. Why had she endured endless bouts of pain and degradation when someone like Jed had been out there waiting for her?

"I have a confession to make, Gracie," Jed said, drooping a chemical-stinking handkerchief over the nostrils of her alligator snout. "I do intend to use your body for something, Grace—but it's not for a painting."

Everything went black.

Chapter Three

The Inflatable Carnival

Denny, the breathless drum turtle massaged his temples beside his two black eyes. When he plumped down on a board beside a chain-link fence outside the carnival gates, his turtle shell resounded with a thunk. "Guys, did any of you happen to grab my inhaler?"

Grace grimaced at the flashing signs of 'DR. PLEASUREDOME'S HALL OF IDENTICAL MIRRORS,' 'WANDA: THE THREE-HEADED PIG,' and 'PHANTOM CAT LADIES' PUSSY FARM (ADULT WOMBATS ONLY).' "Whu—why did you take me back here? You know I used to be a slave in the freakshow here, right?"

Ruffles, the Theremin-playing golden retriever, wagged his tail and barked at his gold ax (Max), flying away high in the air and doing somersaults as if trying to imitate the spiraling pink and blue fireworks overhead.

"I looked at the moon and ran closer to it. I felt like it could save me, or at least calm this burning shapeless hunger the moment I tasted the fresh air of freedom," Reggie the wolf said. He quickly surveyed his surroundings like a shell-shocked veteran. "How long do you think it will take them to find us this time?"

"Oh, fuck," Denny said as his head shrank partway down into his turtle shell.

The black van with '26666666…." painted in white spirals raced into the grass parking lot on the hill, spraying muddy water and giving its shocks a workout as it barreled through potholes and tractor ruts.

Ruffles, oblivious of their plight, barked defiantly at his still floating and glowing golden ax, giving away their position.

Grace roared and tore a hole through the chain-link fence. "C'mon. I know this shitty carnival like my swamp in the Bayou."

"What about Ruffles?" Denny the turtle asked, readjusting his spectacles.

"Forget the mutt. He's so stupid he doesn't know he exists. Besides, he was the only one of us who willingly helped make noise with the 2666 bastards," Reggie said, winking at Grace.

She blushed.

As the members of 2666 greeted Ruffles affectionately and engaged in doggy-talk, the living animal instruments ran past whizzing darts at carny stalls, barns with elementary school art shows, and world's biggest frog competitions.

As they approached the freakshow section, a gold shooting star fell into Reggie's hairy wolf hand. The star was Max the Ax.

Max the Ax smiled until his eyes scrunched up and Reggie could see all the way back to the silver fillings in his molars. "I've always wanted to tell you my ultimate fantasy."

Chapter Four

Max the Ax's Ultimate Fantasy

Max the Golden Ax grew molten hot in Reggie's hairy wolf fist. Max made eyes at Dr. Pleasuredome's Hall of Identical Mirrors. "Take me," Max said, twinkling with gold sparkles, "until the branch of the graveyard tree breaks and falls upon our tombstones."

Reggie and Max ignored the cryptic comment and charged forward. They approached the ticket taker, an old man dressed in a railway conductor uniform. His head tipped back like an antique hand-painted metal toy. Reggie crammed in a few quarters and the gates opened.

Inside the Hall of Identical Mirrors, darkness surrounded them. A spark ignited and sprinted along the mirrors' surfaces. Dim pictures flashed: Max the Golden Ax in a pink frilly cradle; Reggie the wolf screaming in a pink bonnet and chopping off human fingers; and Reggie licking, kissing, and slurping Max the Ax.

"Do you accept the glistening gears of my childhood? It's all pain and darkness now. We have something in common, you know: I used to be a guitar too." Max hopped closer to Reggie and leaned up against his hairy wolf leg. "I lay behind glass. I was the most expensive Les Paul model in the store. Sometimes, people would stand in awe outside the glass but nobody would ever touch or play with me. I saw so many guitars come and go, but nobody wanted to buy me. Nobody wanted to take me home. Was I a leper? A freak?"

Reggie stroked the pickups stitched into his side. He'd

been a prisoner, sure, but hadn't some of those nights felt emblazoned? Supernovas. Stars crashing. Trevor almost fucking him from behind and squirming in ecstasy at the walls and storms of blissful noise cycling and cracking and whipping through implanted wires, but within the veins of his organic wolf circuitry too.

Max bounced up Reggie's arm, resting his blade against the wolf's neck. "I wanted to be a dying comet, not a starfish preserved and bone-dried behind glass. I guess that was when a stoned green witch kid smashed the glass of my case and finally took me away from there. The cops chased him through a foundry where the kid dropped me in a vat of molten gold. When I finally crawled out, I was no longer a guitar. Only the most true and passionate piece of me survived: the golden ax within!"

Three faces appeared in the mirrors painted white, and unmistakably the members of 2666 and Ruffles repeated over and over in the identical mirrors like a loop of terrorizing feedback.

Chapter Five

2 Years Ago
The Disciple's Discipline

Trevor parked his black BMW motorcycle outside the Christmas-themed Halloween party. The skeleton of an elf stared back at him in his rearview mirror.

The music radiating from the house was like nothing he'd ever heard before. Squeals of clipping feedback. Someone mumbling something low and gravelly.

Two girls, wearing leather leotards with devil tongue designs lounged on the front porch huffing a purple smoke through gas masks. "You missed the first band, dipshit," the blonde one said, handing Trevor a bite-marked jade dragon.

Trevor ate the entire dragon's head.

"Whoa, slow down there, tiger," the brunette said, lighting a match on her belt buckle depicting a sinewy naked man holding up the severed head of the devil. She tossed the gas mask aside and lit a cigarette in an ivory holder with Ottoman Turkish script on its side.

Trevor slumped down between them, allowing his fuchsia dragon wings to unfurl and expand behind them.

The humming drone of the noise band inside rose up their spines like a feeling of drifting without gravity through the marble halls of a palace on an alien planet. This was the music Trevor had always wanted to hear. This was the music that had always been missing from Trevor's life. This was a sea in which his spirit could finally boil.

The blonde breathed a blue unicorn, which his fuchsia

snake heads, darting from behind his dragon wings, gobbled up. She slithered beside Trevor and lay her head on his shoulder. "They sacrificed a pig at the end of their last show."

Trevor eased the girls away and turned to gaze inside the house at the scrawny lead singer with greasy black hair, white linen pants, and sweaty, heaving, fish-belly white back kneeling down as if he'd collapsed. There were three barrels behind him. One was labelled 'FISH HEADS,' another 'SAD HEADS,' and a third 'NO HEADS.'

The baby pig squealed and squirmed as the synthesizer player squeezed its midsection, its alarmed expression haunting Trevor as it panicked. The little guy wouldn't stop fighting, so the synth player bashed its head on a cymbal again and again. Finally, its eyes were no longer moving.

Trevor then had the best idea of his life.

Chapter Six

Shark Fin Teeth
1 year ago

Denny, a leatherback sea turtle (and, later, the kick drum of 2666), swam deep and far within the turquoise waters of the Caribbean. Free, powerful, and untethered, Denny heard a siren's call. He was sometimes tempted away from the ocean's depths by the goings-on at St. Barts, Anguilla, or St. Kitts, but this music wasn't Calypso, Reggae, or Soca.

Can you imagine waking up in the brain of a mechanical bird as the entire world is consumed in rainbow flames? Can you imagine schools of tropical fish rushing towards you at once, eager to kiss and caress you into a sleepy hole in the ocean floor? Or try to picture yourself waking up in a cave and all your pink and blue organs have been removed and nailed to the yellow rock wall. Then, when you reach for your insides, the eyes of a lynx emerge behind two candle flames. These were the living dreamlike thoughts of Denny before the incident.

Denny swam closer to to the shore, seduced by the pulsing noise. But it wasn't enough to bob in the dark night ocean waters and strain to hear its dwindling, teasing echoes anymore. He needed to get so close it would burn him. He needed contact. Earth air. All the sea bubbles in the world could never truly touch him. They just popped or swirled away. Then, when the loneliness was breached then soldered shut, he would just lie there, allowing the exploding inside-out tunnel sounds deep into his psyche like a thorn.

He crawled upon the shore of sugary beach sand.

Candles surrounded a circular hut.

Mermaids, buzzed on blue unicorn flesh, lay scissored together around the hut, cobalt blue globs of unicorn flesh dripping down their chins.

"That is so fucking cute. I think he likes the music."

The girl in whale bone jewelry emerged from the hut, her skin tanner than the mermaids, her eyes a ferocious green. She slurped shark fin soup from a wooden bowl.

It was just the drip drop of a desecrated bass buzz. The fusion of multiple sonic maelstroms had only recently abated. Jessie, the drummer of 2666, stormed out, covering Denny in a soft spidery embrace, yet when the sinewy drummer yanked the net taut, Denny realized that the siren's song, in this case, was certainly cursed—particularly when slack-jawed Trevor rose out of the sand dust with the wolf guitar, Reggie wincing in pain and gushing blood from the razor-blade guitar pick and the nonsensical riffs deteriorating into ambient feedback trance seduced the listeners to an ecstatic state of thoughtlessness as he played, plugged into his portable Pignose, and spun like a demonic dervish.

Chapter Seven

Turtle Idols

The three white faces in Dr. Pleasuredome's Hall of Identical Mirrors resembled the members of 2666 less and less. Ruffles pressed his paws against the glass, a pet skeleton seen through an x-ray. His skeleton drooped then dripped like a rapidly burning candle while the reflections of the members of 2666 repeated, retreated, and collapsed into the face of Denny the sea turtle.

"Guys, the band just entered THE HALL. THE hall. the hall—" Denny's words echoed as he disappeared like a ghost.

As if bursting through Denny's green ghost embers, Ruffles growled and lunged at Reggie, ripping off flesh and wolf hair on his knee as he tumbled forward, the mirror flashing and zooming in on the blood pumping from his gash.

Ruffles lunged again, but Max the Ax shot into Reggie's wolf hand like a lightsaber.

Reggie swung Max at Ruffles' head, yet only succeeded in clubbing the mutt's jaw with the ax's underside.

Ruffles, stunned, stepped unsteadily backwards as if seeing stars.

Reggie ran down the hall, made a left, a right, then another left. At the end of the next hall, Ruffles, though bleeding from his gums, had regained composure. He slumped forward menacingly and crawled, growling like a hellhound.

Reggie ran down a different hallway. At the end of this hall was a chute at neck level. He tossed Max up and jumped,

19

but his toe claws scratched the mirror as his hand claws lost their grip on the hard cold surface above. A warm snap followed by a snarl neared his ankle. He kicked wildly and connected with the angry mutt's skull. The kick was more of a stomp than a lunge, and he'd inadvertently managed to get an elbow up onto the rim of the chute. He swung to his right, wedging his curled toes in a corner to propel upwards. Finally, he scrambled into the chute as Ruffles snarled and jumped below.

Chapter Eight

After Reggie crawled for about ten minutes, something wet and slippery touched his furry wolf knees. Had he entered a ceiling vent? He hadn't seen Max's golden glinting form for some time.

He heard dim laughter just ahead.

A man in a wizard cap sat beside two dinosaur birds shaking maracas as a toucan flipped a plate-sized strawberry pancake in a flat pan on an ancient stove.

"Are you shitting me? The band plays on instruments that are alive? Do they play covers?" The wizard snapped his fingers at a napkin holder and 3 chocolate mice crawled out. A scorpion decapitated both mice and spread their bodies onto a piece of toast. The room was filled with pinball machines and arcade games. The wizard spun in his desk chair abruptly. "Noise? They PLAY noise? Is that supposed to be music? Huh? Not at Dr. Pleasuredome's! Who the fuck do you think you're talking to? That's right, you're talking to the doctor himself."

Max bounded down the vent hallway, clattering as he bounced off the sides of the vent. He jumped into Reggie's arms.

Reggie cradled Max soothingly. "Shhh, Max."

Dr. Pleasuredome gazed suspiciously at their exact location in the vent. "Huh? No, sorry. I gotta go. Yeah, ok. If they draw that kind of crowd, book 'em for Friday." He slammed down the phone and shook his wrists until glass swords shot out of them. He lunged beside their location in the vent and, while hovering there, called up two small

21

sharks from a tank on his dresser, They proceeded to chew a hole in the vent, exposing Max and Reggie.

Dr. Pleasuredome eyed Reggie's pickups in his side, but his jaw dropped when he saw Max.

"Max? Is that really you? Where's the rest of your body, my beautiful guitar?"

Chapter Nine

Dr. Pleasuredome decided, since it was a special occasion, that they would all split a can of Bud Light.

"Isn't that just divine? Yeah, that's vintage 1986. I bought it at an ordinary Exxon station here in Virginia." The doc sipped at his champagne glass daintily. "Mmm. The body, the flavor, the aroma, the aftertaste!"

"Jesus. This shit is amazeballs. How did you refrain from drinking it all these years?" Max delicately licked the surface of the rare vintage nectar.

"What's with your friend? Doesn't he talk?"

"Leave him alone. He's been tortured for too long. Ever hear of 2666, the noise band of living animal instruments? Yeah, that's us." Max's ax lips were so small he had to lick so as not to spill any of the godly beverage.

"Funny. I just booked you guys this Friday at the carnival. Still can't believe they would shatter the most beautiful ax I ever did shred Black Sabbath riffs upon into an actual ax. I mean: why?"

"We'd better get going. We quit the band. They were torturing us whenever we played. The band is fucking dead." Reggie downed the rest of his delicious vintage, shuddered in ecstasy at the taste, then got up to go.

The door to Dr. Pleasuredome's office squeaked open.

"Hey, bitches. We got a show to play. Now come back to your master." Trevor dangled Reggie's former choke collar attached to a new set of thicker guitar strings.

"Sorry I fucked you over, guys. I needed the money." Dr. Pleasuredome snapped his fingers and green snakes shot out of his sofa, tying Reggie's wrists and ankles together while others wrapped tightly around Max's handle and ax head. "Here's three free tickets to Tiger Woman's Cheetah Pussy. No hard feelings, okay?"

Chapter Ten

Trevor dragged Reggie by the snake heads knotted around his ankles while nestling Max in his armpit. "Three free tickets to the pussy farm. Well, heh heh. Whattya say, boys? Not like you have a choice." Trevor guffawed, his silver front tooth and werewolf skull belt buckle glinting. "Then we'll roar some noise together. Shredding on a steel and wood ax just feels so wrong. I need you, Reggie." He stroked the empty cord socket in Reggie's side, remembering the warmth and purity of the sound produced by using his wolf body as a guitar. "My fingers and soul will burn before my living altar: you, Reggie."

"But what about Denny and Grace?" Max's voice was muffled by the snake flesh wound tightly around his ax mouth.

They approached Tiger Woman's Cheetah Farm. A woman with dirty blonde hair wearing a cheetah print skirt and neon yellow tights lay her head down on a table as her cigarette burned in a glass claw ashtray.

Trevor slammed the three tickets on the table, knocking the ashtray on the ticket-littered trailer ramp with a smash.

The woman slowly raised her head. She had one red eye and one blue eye and red lipstick stains on her teeth. "You cast a spell on me, silly." She kicked Trevor playfully in the knee then blew ripped rockets into Trevor and Reggie's faces. "Come with me, boys. You need to be warmed by the Cheetah Farm. I remember the noise, Trevor. Let me clean your wounds." She led them inside but it felt more like floating.

Starfish swam through a galaxy on the ceiling as squirrels and chipmunks played crickets like violins. A small collar on the rodents connected them by chain to the crickets. Although the music was cacophonous, they played in perfect sync. Yet as the speed of their playing increased, the crickets shuddered and their round faces flowed to orange and they joined together in a rising scream like 20 singers in a Mozart opera.

The woman's body lay shrunk and ashen, but a majestic glowing cheetah rose above her like a Chinese New Year dragon. She purred and growled. "And just to prove our loyalty." She nodded her head at the squirrels and chipmunks; they pulled the crickets legs until an inky insect blood squirted against their cheeks and their conjoined screams escalated into a spectacular crescendo.

Chapter Eleven

Grace had lost sight of Reggie, Max, and Denny during their mad dash from the other members of 2666. Her determined sprint raced her past the lights, hawkers, and hubbub until she stopped to catch her breath. Then she realized, in horror, that she'd run right back to the freakshow section of the carnival.

Drunken college boys with khakis and white sweaters stumbled out of 'Francis: the Three-Headed Pig;' an old woman with blood dripping from her mouth pounced out of a gate made of skeleton fingers beneath a 'Madame Truffles Web of Delicacies' sign, and a group of serious schoolgirls crawled up from a mud puddle with pink popping bubbles above their heads: scarab divers hooked on poisonous fruit fumes, Grace knew.

But—it couldn't be. The fallen sign reading 'Alligator Girl' in faded garish colors lay beside a collapsed gray silo. Frogheart Jones, his stubby stogie in one corner of his frog mouth, snored with his head titled back. His ruffled satin blazer, once princely, now hung limply, shredded and tattered. At his webbed feet lay his cowboy hat beside a 'Help. My Freak left' sign.

All the memories of pain, torture, and humiliation rushed back until Grace saw purple and she puked her gator human guts out.

"Gracie?" Frogheart's voice travelled as if through a fog. "I knew you'd come back, Gracie." He unbuttoned his fly and exposed his frog genitalia. "Give it your best effort, Gracie. I've been so lonely here without you." He reached to pull her blonde curls, but his face pounded into the ground.

Jed, shirtless and with his spurs glinting, flipped on the cowboy hat and pressed his motorcycle boot into Frogheart's face. "Gracie's too talented for your two-bit flea circus."

"Gracie, no! Please!" Frogheart Jones howled as yellow snot oozed from his frog nostrils.

Jed stomped, mashing Frogheart's face into a steaming pile of mush as his body quivered and quaked. "Welcome back to the band, Gracie. Time to make some noise." Jed smiled like there was more reptile blood running through his veins than hers and Frogheart's combined.

Gracie closed her eyes, wishing she could sink through the earth and fade far away, but also hating herself for the fluttery feeling that rose up when she thought about the screaming fans and the state of ecstasy the synthesizer tones rushing through her body brought on during every single concert and practice session.

Chapter Twelve

Denny had lagged far behind the others during the chase, losing sight of his fellow living instruments shortly after the members of 2666 had arrived at the carnival in their black van.

Huffing and puffing after 12 steps, Denny's turtle foot thudded against an abandoned 'historic well' as the sign read. Dried-out and desperate, Denny plunged down the well, landing in its deep dark waters with a loud plop.

"Denny? Oh Jesus. I'm so sorry. I didn't mean to make fun of you and your family. I'm not a REAL poacher. I would never eat YOU."

As if looking through a wet telescope, Denny could see Jessie, the drummer of 2666, a handsome black man dressed in a white linen suit, with his hands on his knees as he leaned forward and peered worriedly down into the darkness for Denny.

Bubbles rose past Denny's eyes as he shook his head in sadness, recalling all the infinite bashings and ludicrous solos his cracked and chipped shell had endured by mallets, hammers, drum sticks, and, sometimes when the boys were drunk, even Max the Ax—that last one hurt the worst and was the reason for Denny's most threatening crack, which was still gradually rending his shell straight down the middle.

Denny somersaulted underwater and plunged downwards, hoping that wherever this historic well led was deeper than any member of 2666 could ever imagine traveling.

"Denny, we of the deep congratulate you."

"Hello? Who's there?" Bubbles tickled his face as he

swam deeper and deeper.

"You'll become a turtle fireball. Just swim faster and faster. That's right, Denny. Like a comet gathering fire.

"A turtle fireball?"

"Yes, a turtle fireball. Don't you want to save your entire race of leatherback sea turtles from extinction? All you have to do is sacrifice your life. Just come closer to us. Yes, that's right. You'll become a turtle fireball and have revenge on all the poachers, killing their ancestors and progeny with an everlasting fireball. All it requires is your life. Swim deeper, Denny."

Reds and purples surrounded Denny as the waters boiled and webbed hands slapped and pulled him. "No! No!"

Chapter Thirteen

Jessie tied an extension cord to a nearby tree and lowered himself limberly down the well where Denny had disappeared. Muck dribbled down the sleeves of his white linen suit, the extension cord stretched painfully taut in his soft hands. "Denny? Denny, can you hear me? I'm so sorry, Denny. I fucked up real bad. I'm as evil as all the poachers." Jessie's Jesus-sandaled feet touched the gray surface of the well water. "Denny!"

"Denny's with us now, you bastard. His shell's about to break. Nobody can bear to see our shriveled turtle bodies standing outside our shells. Our shells are part of our bodies too, and yet you bashed him while laughing at those animal torture scenes in stupid cannibal movies along with the rest of those bone-headed bozos you call your bandmates. You're going to die. Did you hear me correctly? You and every other poacher, meat-eater, and pet-owner will die by the hands of Denny once he assumes his fireball turtle form and attacks. He's being spun into a weapon a million times more destructive than a nuclear bomb as we speak."

The waters beneath Jessie's feet bubbled and smoked with pinks and reds. Burned slightly, he pulled up a sandaled foot and retreated up the extension cord, yet a warm presence hovered behind him.

Denny, eyes glowing green and flapping wings of fire, drifted closer.

Jessie scrambled up the rest of the extension chord in a mad burst. He collapsed, panting beside the historic well.

Denny's cracked shell fell away. Although shriveled and

deformed-looking without his shell, he stood as straight as he could with his arms crossed while glaring down at Jessie, who scrambled away like a crab, his back slamming into a tree.

Jed dragged a hog-tied Grace into view. He stood beside the tree, speechless at the sight of Fireball Denny who had numerous arms, tails, and wings made of fire surrounding him like a purple electricity ball sold in kid science stores.

Trevor slammed Reggie to the grass beside them. "Now that the band's back together, let's get the fuck out of here. I guess Denny's doing his solo thing."

Chapter Fourteen

Although the members of 2666 cruised at 90 miles per hour, a storm brewed behind them which could not be escaped: the storm of fireball Denny.

Denny's bruised and beaten turtle face swirled in burning clouds like an angry sun god leering down at them.

Jessie, Jed, Trevor, and Ruffles sweated, hearts palpitating hard.

Grace's scales tightened as new muscles emerged under her ribs and in her arms and legs with each breath she took.

Max grew, his wooden ax handle snapping the tightly-wound snakes as his blade extended to Viking proportions.

Reggie's ribs expanded too, pushing against his flesh and hardening into thick muscle.

The wind from inside Denny howled, calling his flames and embers closer to the speeding black van. The highway was deserted. The concrete ramp led them into a tunnel with sparkling tiles on its sides.

Denny followed close behind. All he had to do was think about the band's imminent destruction and, before he could even blink, his body angled into a kill shape, his flames and inner fireball generator accelerating with intensity, a susurration of consequence.

The black van took the next exit off the highway then turned down a road leading through a forest.

Denny lay his cheek on the van's roof, terrified he might start a forest fire and kill all sorts of unsuspecting people and animals--though it was said on many Shenandoah National Park signs that forest fires helped maintain a healthy ecosystem.

The van drove up a gravel driveway on the side of one of the Blue Ridge Mountains.

Jessie, Jed, Trevor, and Ruffles exited the van uneasily, carrying their living instruments precariously as if one false move of unnecessary cruelty could cause Fireball Denny to erupt in a rage, roasting them all in a blanket of flames.

They plugged in their instruments and produced a somber noise, distorted yet muted as they all used soft mallets and gloves. Even Trevor used a violin bow on Reggie and strung him with plastic strings. Yet the human members of 2666 failed to notice the rapid evolution of the living members' bubbling and tightening muscles.

Chapter Fifteen

The practice in the log cabin overlooking the smoky Blue Ridge Mountains had ended around two in the morning. Denny had swirled and drifted around the log cabin, finding the more ambient noise session strangely soothing as his form shifted from a fireball to a dragon shape.

Jed trembled beside Grace in bed. Pale, his cold sweat and coughing suggested he had some type of flu or cold. Grace sensed his sickness, like a malevolent spirit was somehow materially in the room with them.

Jed had dressed Grace in an iron collar and a leather bikini; she resembled a woman on the cover of a sword-and-sorcery paperback. The heavy iron collar was attached to a chain latched to the bed post.

Denny's green eyes glowed through the flimsy white curtain. The faintly charcoal smell of distantly burning forest wafted into the room.

"It wasn't me. I didn't start the fires." Denny's form thinned as he slinked into the room, shifting into a fiery key shape and unlocking the heavy collar, which fell with a loud thunk, waking Jed.

Grace straddled Jed instinctively, her gator tail wrapping around one of his chilly legs like a snake.

Denny sharpened into a burning machete and slipped into Grace's alligator claw behind her scaly back.

Jed smirked. "The gator in you always comes out more when you get turned on." His fingers felt her rough gator skin on her side as he gently fingered some synthesizer keys to test the volume of the amplifier. The church organ synth tones sounded like a summoning. His eyes rolled back in his head as he continued to make hypnotic noise.

"Kill him. cut his throat," came a voice in Grace's head.

"Denny? is that you?"

"Forget about Denny. he's a magic wand in your hand. Can't you feel him burning there? He wants you to kill. Remember what he said to you in the pool at the noise fest in Florida after he showed you real pleasure for the first time in your life?"

Jed smiled, then gasped, pressing a few keys down on the curve of Grace's lower back as he squeezed her hard scaly breast.

Grace let go of Denny the burning knife and fitted the iron collar to Jed. As it locked with a click, he said, "I'm lost in a trance with you. I never want to come back."

She clicked the other end to her ankle, wrapping her body around Jed's face while feeling weightless, making out with a memory of Denny when they were buzzed on unicorn flesh in a motel pool in Florida and then feeling the bristly reality of Jed's mustache as she pulled his greasy hair, willing him to die as she shuddered and ground her throbbing jeaned groin against his pink wet lips, skin flaps separating like reptilian blood could loosen bones from flesh.

Chapter Sixteen

Trevor lay in bed beside Jessie as they watched Denny's green eyes circle the log cabin. The faraway fires on a facing Blue Ridge Mountain appeared like lava trickling down its side, overlapping the flames of Denny like stained glass.

Jessie sat up in bed and lit a Camel with a match. The sheets were draped over his legs, his light black skin smooth, silky, and decorated with black and purple tattoos. One of his tattoos depicted a human-headed woman nursing a baby turtle. A compartment in the chest section of her shell opened from which jutted a human breast. The breasts of the tattoo figure lined up exactly with Jessie's nipples.

"If you knew the exact date of your death, would that change how you lived your life?"

Trevor stopped pacing and joined Jessie, placing an arm around him. "Still upset about Denny, huh?"

Jessie leaned on Trevor's bare shoulder. "I want to enter the body of a wild stallion leaping off a cliff at the exact second when my heart stops beating." Jessie took a long drag on his Camel until a clump of ash fell on his thigh, singeing a hair.

Trevor swiped the cigarette and slumped back, staring upwards at the slowly rotating ceiling fan.

"Or I'd want to be a sea turtle too. I'd make it up to him somehow, deep down at the bottom of the ocean. Save his family from poachers." Jessie sighed and strutted naked to the window, his half erect cock slapping against his thighs.

Denny's glowing green eyes hovered closer and closer to the window as his dragon fire body coiled up behind him like malfunctioning fireworks.

"I'm so sorry, Denny. I just want you back in the band."
Jessie only whispered. The glass between them rippled,
cracked, and blackened as if from a blow torch.

Denny blushed.

Jessie was fully erect, pressed against the cool window
in longing.

"We eat you, we pet you, and we play you, but we need
you in our lives, Denny. Won't you ever come back?"

Jessie leaned into the window, cracking the glass
completely as Denny rushed forward until he filled the tattoo
in Jessie's chest like a conjoined baby sea turtle twin, no
longer flamed but reptile-fleshed and spotted-shelled.

Chapter Seventeen

Max couldn't sleep either because of the purple guitar in the corner of the room.

Ruffles, the golden retriever, snoozed away in his bassinet.

The purple guitar arched its back and crawled over to Max, who was in a leather holster beside Ruffles's groin.

"Nikki?" Max leaned his ax head against the spiraled side of the purple guitar.

"Hello, Max. I heard your sadness call to me from another world. I lay with snail creatures in a pink desert beside a hovering iguana. We were about to be married when you broke through to me. You calm me, even now. My pincers, my fangs, and my insect thorax grew back inside. The sky cracked and poured a sizzling purple liquid over me, reassembling me to my former ax shape as I came crawling back to you, my love. But do you even remember me?"

"Remember you? You were the only one to ever be placed beside me in the glass case in the music store. Why did they keep us in that prison, never allowing us to mingle and get to know the other instruments?"

Nikki used her strings to slide Max out of the holster on Ruffles's groin and to slice through the snakes that bound him. "We belonged to the beautiful ones once. We belonged to famous musicians who could never seem to last. Don't you remember your original master? The one who played you until the sun and the moon fell in love and they killed the world?"

Ruffles twitched in his sleep, scratching his groin and

narrowly missing slicing Nikki with a paw nail.

"He's a pet. You're an ax who used to be a guitar, but were you ever an animal?" Nikki said, chewing through the last of the snake binds. "I used to be a whale and then a shark before I drifted into a tree. I got stuck there for centuries before they harvested me and made into a prince's guitar." Nikki's purple guitar body moved like clay. He moved closer to Ruffles's mouth. "And so the ultimate revenge and gift would be to free him of his petdom slavery and turn him into an ax like the two of us." Nikki charged down Ruffles's throat.

Ruffles's eyes shot open in terror, his paws extending as he howled in pain. His choke collar fell to the floor, burning to molten gold. His skin turned purple as he shifted from dog to werewolf, guitar strings falling from his gums like spider webs until they reached his toes, wound around each digit, and stretched taut.

"You've got a show tomorrow night," the purple werewolf guitar roared. "Better start practicing."

Chapter Eighteen

A bloody bandage begged to be ripped from the wall hung in the kitchen where 2666 had been practicing the previous evening. Although it was now 5 in the morning, all the old members and new members were drawn to the scent of the spot like the ferocious glance of someone who wants you as bad as you want them.

Jessie, with Denny growing out of the turtle tattoo on his chest, was the first to arrive. He lay on his back on the kitchen floor. Denny, half submerged in his nipple, rose up and gently slapped his skin like a seasoned tabla player.

At first, Jessie's face relaxed as though he were receiving a massage. Gradually, however, Denny's slapping increased in intensity, becoming more of a pounding and as if directed at Jessie's pressure points. He tried swatting at Denny growing from his tattoo, but the skin surrounding Denny grew porous and cracked, aching and threatening to rend.

"What? Don't you like to be played?" Denny's slapping became furious, the veritable madness of a psychedelic rock drummer destined to die early.

Low laughter seeped from the bloody bandage. "Rip me off the wall! Rip me off the fucking wall." Her voice was smoky as her bandage body bunched up into a smile and rose petals dribbled from her mouth. As the ghost of the bandage emerged above, her skin a thick smoke the color of marshmallow, she rolled out onto the floor like a gallon of spilled milk and pulled her silky being inward into a 40s noir harlot reclining and smiling deceptively. She splashed herself into a flying carpet shape down a hall and brought

41

back Trevor playing Reggie.

Trevor played, uncharacteristically, neither noise, drone, nor feedback loops but rather a song with Django Reinhart style picking. Reggie was plugged into a small Pignose amplifier, which floated on a blue cloud beside them.

Reggie winced in pain as Trevor strummed with his razor blade finger picks, frequently slicing into the skin surrounding and beneath the pickups embedded into his stomach's rows of stitches like the ones on Frankenstein's monster's forehead.

Something sharp bit into Reggie's hind leg: it was a purple werewolf guitar beside floating Max. As Reggie felt the full moon grow closer and the ghost of the bloody bandage whisper in his ear to "leak into me, you unloved dirty sow," he plucked off a guitar string from his body like floss with newfound godly strength.

Chapter Nineteen

Reggie plucked off one twisty guitar string and then another, jamming the ends into Trevor's forehead. He squealed and tried to scratch out Reggie's eyes with his razor-blade fingerpicks. He tore a pickup from his stomach and proceeded to ram it into Trevor's side without removing his Wolf Eyes t-shirt.

Trevor screamed and thrashed, yet Reggie's muscles continued to bulge and grow. The purple werewolf guitar drooled beside him. At the eclipse of Trevor's screams, as Reggie tied guitar strings to Trevor's teeth, toes, balls, and ears, Nikki, the purple werewolf guitar who inhabited and had transformed Ruffles, moved closer to Reggie, running a paw down his treasure trail and stroking him as she purred "more, more!"

But the first rays of the sun had already began cascading through the blinds and open windows, depleting both Nikki and Reggie of their werewolf strength. Yet the task had been completed: at Reggie's feet lay the fully-strung Trevor, a perfectly usable and functioning human guitar.

Chapter Twenty

Grace dragged Jed by his iron collar, but he would not budge off the bed. His eyes had a glassy look and his tongue jutted out stiffly.

A variety of musical styles resounded down the hallway as the sun rose, including opera, classical symphonies, and devilish fiddle music along with a healthy helping of disco, of course.

Although immensely talented visionaries, Grace had only ever heard 2666 produce noise or ambient music—never anything following rules or order. She found the current medley of conventional styles oddly discomforting. And yet she needed to be part of it. The other end of the iron collared chain, however, was still clamped around her gator ankle.

Grace dragged Jed down the hallway to the kitchen as the sun rose and the smoke from the fires burning on the Blue Ridge Mountains made the orange light heavy and hazy.

Only the faint playing of a piano could be heard as Grace dragged Jed down the endless hallway.

Grace entered the kitchen and noticed a banner—like a happy birthday banner but it said:

HEY GRACE, WE THOUGHT YOU WERE DEAD SO WE LEFT TO SET UP FOR THE SHOW AT THE CARNIVAL TONIGHT.

Jed groaned then smacked his lips, wetting his tongue. "What happened? Where am I? Where is everybody?"

A woman with a deep voice—the ghost of the bloody bandage—giggled. She coalesced like a cloud as the fires burned on the trees outside the log cabin window. Black smoke billowed against the glass, cracking it lightly.

Jed's truck was parked in the driveway. The synthesizer amp had already been loaded and strapped down.

Jed grasped his knee. One of Grace's synthesizer keys must have fallen off her gator tail. He tried to pull it out but whined in agony when it refused extraction. Blood lightly trickled down his shin. "How could you do this to me, Gracie? Pull it out. Pull it out!"

Grace picked up a pair of pliers from a side table and viciously ripped a synthesizer key from her scaly side. "What? This?" She held the synth key inches from his face, shaking it angrily until his face was flecked with her blood and his nose was knicked from the metal stitch end jamming into him. Grace picked up a wooden cutting board, lay the offending synth key on Jed's side, and used the board like a hammer. "We have to get ready for the show, Jed honey."

Jed screamed.

"We promised the crowd living instruments, but it's you we'll play tonight."

Chapter Twenty-One

The carnival was mostly deserted by the time Grace rolled up with squealing Jed the human synthesizer while Marla, the ghost of the bloody bandage, tended to his wounds by plugging his gashes up with her smoky body and leaking unicorn flesh into his brain.

Yet as the dust settled and they'd parked, a spirited drum-kit made of painted turtles and snappers played by a free-jazz wolf-headed human drifted into view. He wore a silk blue suit as he whistled to himself and gazed deep into the fires burning on the Blue Ridge Mountains. He squeezed the ass of a chicken suspended from a pole above a cymbal for his finale, producing a series of tortured squawks.

"Have you seen 2666?" Grace shouted from the cab of Jed's truck, but, although he then made eye contact, the wolf drummer did not respond and began anew with his aggressively unpredictable racket as if drinking from a renewable well of inspiration.

Three turtles with bubbly eyes emerged from a hole in the kick-drum. They lowered a rope made of tied-together pants (each of these turtles had human-shaped legs) and one after the other, they climbed down the ladder wearing only tighty whitie underwear and their turtle shells like coats.

After they'd descended, they glanced wistfully at the drum set, where a variety of live turtles were screwed, bolted, and fastened into place.

"Hey guys? Whatcha doing?" The wolf said, his tongue hanging out of the side of his mouth as he panted. "Soup time." He did a flip over the front of the drums and scooped up the three turtles in a single movement. He returned to his drummer's seat, unscrewed one of the stands until a snapping turtle's cymbal shell turned over and filled with boiling water, smelling of chicken bouillon. "Mmm. Wish this was gator soup." His gold front tooth gleamed as he leered at Grace's trembling reptile thighs.

"Don't you dare." Grace held the wolf in rapt attention as he held the three crying turtle children above the soup. She looked imposing with her alligator tail swatting back and forth, a chain still connected from her ankle to Jed's neck.

The drummer wolf threw the weeping turtles against a nearby shed, smashing them to their deaths. "Well lookie here. A live crocodile synthesizer with reptile-manitarian intentions. By the time I'm through with you, you'll be begging for it again through broken gator fangs."

Before Grace could dispute this, the limber wolf was again flipping through the air. He dragged Grace to the nearby shack along with the amp from the back of the truck and plugged her in, playing her with the adeptness of Wendy Carlos.

Grace screamed and fought but the athletic wolf smushed her face into the dirt with his hairy clawed foot until she could no longer breathe. Just as she was about to pass out, she glanced over at the smashed turtle kids and swore she saw a twinkling light of hope.

Chapter
Twenty-Two

The little turtles who had been tossed to their deaths rose up from their smashed bodies as blue ghosts. They held hands and surrounded the outlet where the athletic wolf had plugged Grace in. Blue and purple vines of electricity ran up and down their little blue bodies from the outlet. They descended and chewed the synthesizer cord.

Grace felt a surge of energy and pushed the athletic wolf off her back.

A purple and blue version of her made of surging electricity and lightning bolts stood before her. "Get out of the way." Her electricity self pushed her gator self aside. It embraced the athletic wolf then gave a little hump into his groin, sending him stumbling away dumbly and blackening until he fell to the ground motionless, burned to a crisp, and faintly smoking.

"Thank you guys. I'm sorry I couldn't save you in time." Graced wiped sweat off her brow.

Jed, still connected to her ankle, coughed from the rising dust in the grassy parking lot.

"We want to go home. Back to our drum set." But the turtle children were fading from existence.

Electric Grace held the vanishing blue turtles.

"I'm sorry guys, but maybe you'll come back to life in some other form."

The turtle children floated and faded, the sun emerging from a cloud overexposing their existence.

As the dust settled further, Grace saw that the carnival parking lot was completely full. The distant screams of terrified delight from brave ride-goers, sugar-rushed toddlers, horny high-schoolers, and the laughter of small towners delight and surprise as they donned goofy mushroom hats and drifted towards Grace and Jed.

A number of passersby, however, gawked at the sight of Grace (the Gator woman) dragging a sickly Jed by a chain connecting his neck to her ankle.

An overweight man chewing the stub of a cigar sat on a stool at the carnival's entrance, his gut blending in with his groin. "Fie dollahs." He spat an enormous clump of green phlegm into the dirt.

Grace hummed until a quiet scream emerged and a variety of ghost turtle kids crawled out of Grace's eyes as if from behind wallpaper and decorated the ticket taker with jewels, makeup, sandalwood perfumes, and exotic ornaments from around the world. After they were finished, the man had tree limbs and was dressed in a tuxedo but wearing lipstick, earrings, and just enough rouge.

"Go right ahead, miss." He bowed, smacking his lipstick lips.

Where there had been dust and yellow grass, a purple velvet now grew in the areas he directed.

Chapter Twenty-Three

Grace dragged Jed down the midway by the chain.

Jed, pale and wheezing, sometimes crawled and sometimes lay limp through the dust of stroller wheels, electric wheelchairs, cowboy boots, and sandals—while Grace pulled him by the collar around his neck over muddy cardboard boxes used like planks over puddles.

Jed's most recent coughing fit forced Grace to stop and kneel down beside him. "Stop. Look." The horses on his polyester cowboy shirt ran off the threads and into his hand. The horses were kicking and struggling. "Give me your hand."

The crowd kept stumbling over them, almost tripping.

An ornery hick in overalls with a front tooth missing began to lecture them.

Jed passed the horses into Grace's scaly gator claw and they were absorbed into her skin."They'll gallop into your heart and kiss like melting sherbert rainbows."

She pulled Jed gently by his chain.

"Get back to the fucking freak show where you belong." The hick's voice was drowned out by the surging crowd but he continued to stare, staining them with a sense of guilt until the blue turtle children appeared and slammed him with a purple wand. Dazed, he peeked out of a purple velvet cushioned stage coach as his beautiful blonde hair floated behind him like a bridal train and he blew kisses exploding into unicorn flesh gummies.

The red horses under the scaly skin of Grace's hand pulled her past a few tents, between them, and onto a different path where only a drunken clown with smudged face paint lay beside a unicorn head with its face chewed off.

Posters representing black silhouettes of human instruments played by animals on a yellow background hung from the sides of tents advertising the show tonight of 2666.

The concert was to be held at Jester's Pavilion, a structure next to the Freakshow. Yet why were the humans being played as instruments by animals? Shouldn't it be the other way around?

Jed shook, his eyes glassy as he writhed on the dirt path as if having a premonition at a séance. "But you're never going to have any kids of your own. You'll die too soon." Jed's lips had a dirt mustache. An apple growing a head of hair hovered beside his face with a list of obligations Grace was meant to attend to. "And you're never going to see your parents again. They're trapped in an igloo at the bottom of the bayou."

Grace sobbed while kneeling beside Jed, holding his callused hand and murmuring "I forgive you. I forgive—" until a blunt object hit the back of her head and her vision faded to black.

Chapter Twenty-Four

When Grace woke it was night and she was on a stage, restrained by a black leather muzzle, green velvet booties tickling her gator claws, and plugged into an amplifier. The stars above twinkled in slow motion as if their fires were pyres for lost loved ones.

A hushed crowd of thousands surrounded the pavilion. The crowd swayed gently as Jed dug a spiked finger into her side, the whoosh of the synthesizer rushing through Grace's body as he jammed a key, forcing a sustained note that pricked at the blood flowing through her reptile veins.

Jed's neck was still attached by a chain to Grace's ankle as he climbed into a porcelain bathtub with gold lion's feet on the stage. A bunch of contact mikes had been set up inside. He crawled inside without Grace, stretching the chain taut as he gasped for air and his face turned bluish and he relayed a bizarre monologue while spraying cleaning fluid on a sponge and paper towels. "Grace, I gotta clean our tub. There's a bit of mildew in here, but there's nothing but love for you in my art. I sweat and strain and burn because of you, baby. I'll exterminate the dirt and microscopic poisons to clean our souls, honey. I'm down on my hands and knees working until the poisonous sweat of my soul pours out. And after it's clean, fall down with me through the drain to the dark ocean waters, past the bioluminescent blues of sea life, the ball-shaped fish bodies containing little fish heads like seeds, and the neon red scavenger snakes chewing fallen whale carcasses. Let's get lost in the microscopic bacteria on a whale bone, baby."

Grace batted her heavy eyelashes.

Reggie, as muscular as a superhero comic book werewolf, had chopped off Trevor's head and stitched it to his groin. He squeezed a black silk sack containing his genitals as he strummed the bloody strings wound around Trevor's teeth like barbwire floss. Tears streamed down his thighs as the blue ghosts of turtles flew, drying his tears with their angelic bat wings until they landed on the shoulder of Denny's shell, who beat an enormous kick drum mercilessly inside of which Jessie flipped and jumped, his face pulled into a rat-like formation, his limbs tied to a series of levers and pumps like an abused ventriloquist dummy.

Grace flipped to her hands and knees and pulled viciously at the chain, slamming Jed's forehead into a side of porcelain which sent a ragged ripping sound through the contact mikes as the tub split down the middle as though the leaking blood were the thing corroding it as it cracked.

"It was all for you, my love. I scrubbed away all the grime and the insects. Even the last traces of your alligator blood." He reached a mildewed, moldy hand towards Grace.

She ripped synthesizer keys from her side, jabbing them into Jed with mad abandon. He shrieked, crawling away on his hands and knees hysterically.

Grace ran across the stage, shaking her wild greasy hair like she was channeling a demon and pumping its fury into the music. The crowd was quiet but held in rapt attention. Finally, she pounced on Jed in a prehistoric movement, ripping off Jed's legs while smiling and laughing as blood and synthesizer keys poured down her plated chest and erect nipples, her plated gator tits gleaming in the slick sheen of her dead lover's blood.

Chapter Twenty-Five

The carnival show—and final concert—of 2666 echoed for over a decade afterward in photographs, dream capsules, nightmares, fantasies, and even under the eyelids of all your secret crushes, and in the underwear of your best friend's girl.

One could often find it projected at backyard parties when the rodent cops went to sleep and unicorn flesh was consumed.

Some called it bloodshed, terror, a ghostly rainbow, being trapped inside a diamond while cumming blood, angry hair, ferocious jaws, etc.

You see: each of us insects were blessed in our own ways. Our parents cherished our every hairy insect limb and misshapen mandible. And when we quaked in fear, yes our hair did flop back and forth like someone hysterically shaking a mop. And we were the ones really controlling it all. We were the microscopic ones on both the human and animal instruments, so it was really us playing them all along.

We'd been singing to the humans through so many lives, through violin-like legs when we were crickets, with peeps and ribbeting when we rode frogs, with chirping and endless song when we flew on the backs of birds, and with zaps and electronic squeals when we burrowed into the skin of aliens in outer space, their infected limbs floating through the atmosphere like neon candy.

That was the part that nobody understood: we were calling to you, you humans. And this is our song. We're playing through you. We are the thunder in your brains and the ticks in your hearts. You are the instruments of our destructive tendencies.

What? Do you hear that sound? That rustling, silky sound? That's the atmosphere making love with the scruff of a thousand years of unwanted refuse in the form of tears from sleep-crusty eyes of an ant being swallowed by a cockroach gliding upon a spider's wings.

We inhabit the animal and human planets floating down the k-hole pupils of dead unicorns: we, the animal human insect bands.

Chapter Twenty-Six

Epilogue

"Yes, those were some foggy years, Denise." She turned off her phone and adjusted her sunglasses, frowned, and returned her attention to her enthusiastic son, claws tugging at her red leather skirt. Scars at the corners of her lips gave the impression that her face could never truly beam with genuine happiness.

"Mommy! Look! A wolf guitar! Can I get one? Please!? I always wanted to play the ax. Dun dun. Dun-anunnu dun-dun." Klaus mimicked playing the guitar, spittle flying this way and that.

The drugged, sour-looking wolf in the packaging pressed meekly against the plastic as if ready to bestow his last dying breath to a wounded maiden, admitting he had failed in his fairy tale quest.

Grace, still a gator on the inside, removed her samurai sheath and sliced her son Klaus down the middle, freeing the wolf and quickly stringing up the halves of her son with steel guitar strings, struggling to retain a grip on each of his slippery halves hopping away from the other. She ripped out the input jack from the trembling, traumatized wolf and rammed it into her son's belly button and made him a double ax..

Grace turned the volume up to 1,000, shredding on her son the ax as her alligator soul rose high above the world like the smoke from a nuclear bomb and she prayed, becoming one with the animal lords of noise and all of their insect progeny.

Nicholaus Patnaude

Skeleton
Glass

There was a time when getting lost could inspire hellish panic, cold sweats, and pulsing visions of snarling rodents washed out in the flash of headlights.

My summer driving a delivery truck at my uncle's lumber company contributed to this crippling phobia.

For 10 years afterwards, I feared driving on highways or for extended periods. My grip would tighten on the steering wheel as Uncle Nick playfully covered my eyes with his soft white clown gloves again.

***

"Why is there still lumber in your truck?" Uncle Nick's voice echoed in the vast lumber barn.

"They were closed." Sweat dripped down my sides. The table saw rumbled, hungry to devour more cedar planks.

"Are you joking?" He stared at me with his double pupil in one eye, the result of a nail gun accident.

"I got lost."

He put on his white gloves. "You drove all the way to Madison on company time and didn't make the delivery?"

"I'll go back tomorrow. I'll work on Saturday."

"Unbelievable." He flicked a menthol cigarette at an overflowing ashtray beneath a picture of Kathy Ireland squeezing limes against her neon nipples. "Un-fucking-believable."

A tear fell to my dusty hands.

He stormed off into the dark corner of the lumber barn. The table saw soon resumed squealing and shredding powdery sprays of sawdust drifted through the air.

My parents' house was on the same piece of property as the lumber company and my uncle's house.

I spent most of my time in a moldy basement during my parents' divorce. I'd sing and close my eyes, becoming the

61

lead singer in a wild goth band. I'd paint my face in clown makeup, waiting for the freak train in my underground bedroom.

"All aboard!" a limbless conductor would shout. "Don't have the fare?" He snorted a pink bean from the controls into his nostrils. "Rumor has it you're set to play Madison Square Garden tonight. Better get a move on, buster. And the children want to know--" He opened a toy box with the tip of his worm tail; it contained three gasping gummy spiders, their human teeth grinding together between his teeth as his lips smacked. "They want to know if you'll be playing 'Skeleton Glass,' your 70s hit?"

Only my blacklight continued to burn overhead. Scary drawings, LPs, loose tobacco, and black candles surrounded me. I had to work on constructing a mask they would never forget.

"Yeah," I said, keeping the nightmare blue. "I'll play 'Skeleton Glass' for the kids. And for the fans who've stuck by me since the beginning."

***

People whispered behind my back and posted my face over the naked female manikin with removable organs the next Monday in health class. The scent of formaldehyde wafted up from the creatures pinned to the blue wax of the dissection pans.

The lights went off for a few seconds. My sparkling skeleton glass belt buckle dazzled them all.

Tiffany chewed her pencil absently, lazily parting her thighs while grasping the hem of her khaki skirt. Her blazing white panties melted like milk; the lips of her sex gasped in sync with the mouths of the creatures pinned to the pans.

When I tiptoed to the front of the class to retrieve a tissue from the teacher's desk, a tiny elevator opened beside the trash can. Tiffany continued to part her legs and slap her thighs together in the silvered reflection of the shiny trash can. Torture was something you could suck through a straw while drinking the skin of tangerines and mangoes.

A frog with deer legs walked through the opened elevator doors once an hour or so, carrying a stack of pies and a steaming cup of tea. He wanted to be sure he was "never late for skeleton class" so he would "never be dissected" like his "brothers" (the frogs in the dissection pans) as he continually reminded me, sneaking a glance at Tiffany's gasping vulva which opened wider as he glared at it, puckering and spitting, her clitoris reddening and engorging as if in communication with his frog flesh.

"We must battle the humans, our enemies, until every last one of them is buried in their stinking graves. Look at her maddened frog flesh, battling to once again fade to glorious green against her weak and pink human reproductive organs." The frog eyed me suspiciously, then returned his complete attention to Tiffany.

The skin on her face stretched out of shape, her smile lengthening to ghoulish proportions as her body drooped below the black counter of the lab table like a rubber suit.

"Want to go down there and finger me while your girlfriend watches?" Mrs. Hupert, wearing a white lab coat and square black glasses, said, motioning towards Tiffany's steaming pile of green and black-spotted flesh. Mrs. Hupert licked her lips and raised her radiation goggles to her forehead. Her skin was burned as if from direct beach sun. Sweat cascaded down her temples. "Maybe your tongue can be a roasting spit and burn me on the inside."

Mrs. Hupert was usually distant and cold, yet when we hugged her body tightened then softened like an uncoiled spring turning to jam, a skeleton in full chrysalis.

***

I turn on the radio. Some gloomy French troubadour sings of cigarettes and broken hearts as you lie back naked on your bed, Tiffany. The flowers I pinned to your wrists and thighs wilt as we recall Brian's goth mullet and the laser lights from the limo's bar on the way to prom, then drinking beer from the headmaster's cup award at the afterparty. You blew me after we moved phone books and rotary phones from a bed with a quilt, your femur bones and hips a white lightning fluid pumping through your reptile makeup. There were fireworks in your hair as you sang and danced to Françoise Hardy. You rubbed the grip of your Ruger .38 special down your silver sequined panties and made me lick the juices. The urges slither through me. I relax. I close my eyes. I drive by your house. I'm grateful for all our days as I drip from your mirrored sunglasses in the locked rooms of lost memories. The soft clown gloves of Uncle Nick grasp my neck and push down, but I'm so serene I can breathe underwater. I drip molten skeleton glass about to crystallize. I'm confident about driving now. I'm the perfect driver, a crystal driver. I can even go to sleep as my crystal body drives for me. I melt through the back of my seat and find Uncle Nick suffocating under a purple web of skeleton glass. I remove his white clown gloves and cover his eyes with them this time. If only you could still be here with me, Tiffany. If only you weren't in the car with Brains and me on that rainy night through Skeleton Class. I can chase us all backwards with my purple crystal skull.

Maybe it was only natural that I'd later become an EMT. On my first night, there was a head-on collision resulting in a double fatality. We had to cut a guy's legs off to remove him from his vehicle with bolt cutters. One of his legs was stuck. The tow truck driver refused to move the truck with the severed leg still in the cab, so I had to wrench it loose with a tire iron. We strapped the leg to a gurney and brought it to the hospital. They put the leg in a body bag all by its lonely self.

I drove home with blood on my white uniform, but it was a few months later when Brains spoke to me through another victim; a steering wheel had crushed through this victim's chest. As soon as we used the jaws of life to pull him out, he'd fallen apart. What killed him also held him together. It was a lot like skeleton glass.

"You fucked up big time. We travelled through skeleton glass to skeleton class," the victim croaked in the voice of Brian Brains, "just to reach you. We can be with you for as long as you like, but the purpling glass will shatter if you try to touch us."

***

I turned on the radio the night of the accident too. One of my headlights burned out in my Mazda, so my mother let me take her skeleton glass hearse to meet up with Tiffany and Brains.

But before I met with them outside Madison Square Garden to sing 'Skeleton Glass' at my farewell show, I had an unpleasant errand to run. I'd decided to tell my uncle that I wasn't going to work for him anymore, that it was unhealthy for family members to work together, and that there would be no two week's notice because I might wake up to find him shaking my bed like he had last Saturday morning, then reaching to cover my eyes with his clown gloves.

I drove down the dirt road on our family plot past a nervous rabbit and a hick on his tractor who rented my Uncle Nick's nearby duplex; the hick puttered by and waved, a glint of purple starlight briefly burning in his eyes. If I ever made it to my concert that evening, I'd unfold velvet flowers in my voice.

I rounded the bend and dipped down, skidding through a mud puddle in the gravel. Growing up, I always wanted our enormous driveway to get paved but my uncle would just shovel loose gravel into the potholes whenever they got washed out. I could've walked there, but the mosquitoes were ferocious at this point in the summer due to the 30 acre swamp on the family plot.

Uncle Nick's skeleton glass Harley was covered in clear plastic garbage bags and spider webs. Hungry and horny, the glass leaked fuchsia sparkles and melted from the heat.

I walked inside and knocked on the already open door to his living room. A lone mosquito coasted with its hair-like mandibles extended.

"Uncle Nick?" A baby monitor on the kitchen table issued a fuzzy screeching sound. I sat down and turned up its electrical-taped volume knob; a field recording from an alien planet issued from its speaker. It swirled and swirled into a sonic maelstrom, its alluring tone eroding rational thought, depositing me on static branches of glowing ivy on a purple planet where Brains pinned a naked Tiffany to a dissection slab, his flaccid cock dragging across her stomach as he retrieved nails from his jockstrap and pushed them into her limbs.

"Welcome to the wheel!" My uncle Nick dressed as a witch with purple skin hovered above them on his broomstick, his black velvet cloak whipping in the wind. "Nail her good. I don't want her squirming in her seat during skeleton class." The room transformed but was too bright to display the new contours.

***

I turn up the radio and turn off the headlights, drifting to the rhythm of Brain and Tiffany's heartbeats as though they were the electronic bass line from a song about our lost youths.

***

The light on the baby monitor blinked. "[static] Eric? [static] What the hell are you doing here [static]? You should be out on a delivery! Why the fuck is your truck still stacked with sheet rock and lumber?" The baby monitor's one blinking light stared back like a cyclops. "When you go out on a delivery, you make the delivery. Am I speaking Espanol? Tu Hables Espanol?"

"Uncle Nick?" I tiptoed into the dining room. The lights burned brightly, glinting off the glass cabinets filled with my deceased grandmother's collection of ceramic clowns.

"Why aren't you laughing?"

I turned the knob all the way to the left. The baby monitor clicked off and became still. "Is anybody there?"

A cold wave of feverishness grazed the top of my hand like a breeze. Cold as skeleton glass is the witch's hand when it pulls off the white gloves in the barn and the lumber burns.

***

"Do you want to talk about what you saw, Eric? Why are you shaking?"

My mother hadn't been the first one to suggest I quit driving for awhile, but she'd been the most supportive. Both of her legs were propped up on a brown leather ottoman because of complications with her knee surgeries. "Do you want to watch a movie with me, Honey?"

We watched old Japanese movies mostly, but I could not see beyond the pictures in my mind to the forlorn samurai on the television.

My wounds throbbed under the bandages as I struggled to forget the image of Tiffany's face splashed against her panties and the windshield as Brain's overgrown head opened like a tin can and led us through the doors to skeleton class. Push away the dead frogs and fuck me, Eric. There's broken bits of skeleton inside me. Bend with my spine through the funnel of night.

***

I had to accept it, or at least tell someone about it, but like a victim of sexual abuse the words atrophied in my throat.

"Do you want to talk about what you saw, Eric?" The green leather of Dr. Smertz's couch slithered like a sleepy snake as I drifted off to skeleton class.

Yes, Dr. Smertz. I do want to talk about my driving-related phobias with you. But, alas, the good doctor Smertz too is gone with the flickering of the years. I've tried pills, bottling the drugs, and shooting up fireflies. I've scented heathen and sinister. I've burned across brains through cool tin and rippling brimstone, fogging from her sighs and the turbulence of our needs.

My hands grip the steering wheel intensely. Trees surround me. I drive in lost circles. I hyperventilate. Patches of time disappear. Then I return to another part of the circle: the deer's legs stick up from a dirt mound in the forest. They are hairy light brown with tufts of white fur and hoofed. But they are shaped like human's legs. And somewhere a solitary leg is still strapped down to a gurney.

I drive forward with my eyes closed, hoping to cause a crash through skeleton glass. One damned gateway for me alone. Cicadas silence my screams in the spring when my face gets covered over by a bees nest. I pull over and park mom's purple glass hearse, the alien glass rippling like bugs skate within it. I park it next to a wooden shack with a hand-painted sign on which is scrawled 'SKELETON CLASS' in white paint. I'm cut up from all the glass and the crash as the jaws of life machine beeps while backing up and I readjust my neck cast.

I enter the one-room classroom.

Uncle Nick draws a map on the chalkboard with pink and blue chalk.

Brian Brains and Tiffany sit behind wooden desks wearing Catholic school uniforms. A series of wires connect the hem of Tiffany's skirt to Uncle Nick's eyelashes; each time he blinks, he pulls her flannel skirt higher. Transparent sea creatures float around the room.

"These aren't sea creatures, actually. They're Skeleton Glass." Tiffany's breath smells like strawberry gum. The gold cross hanging between her exposed cleavage rises and falls with her slight gasps. "So you finally decided to follow the mouse and complete the route to collect the loot of skeleton glass. That's great. I'm so happy you're finally here. We missed you!" She leans forward to kiss me but her skirt is ripped off by Uncle Nick's eyelashes.

Brains pulls off his white dress shirt and blushes. He picks at a boil on his elfish ear, his black hair grown long and greasy. He rocks a cradle containing a severed leg. "Wanna tuck her in?"

Uncle Nick wipes the perspiration from his forehead with a silk purple and black handkerchief.

House centipedes crawl up Tiffany's legs and chew through her panties.

Uncle Nick draws in pink and blue chalk a series of spirals of interconnected routes and what exits to get off on certain highways to avoid weigh stations or traffic jams. The chalk's color mirrors the blue of Tiffany's veins.

***

I leave the one-room classroom and return to my mother's

skeleton glass hearse. Something warm drips on my shoulder. I'm bleeding through the bandages again.

The deer legs kick wildly. My mother's smoking hearse is turned over. I howl outside it, finally freed from the rigid loop. One skeleton glass wheel still spins.

I reach a bloodied hand through the mist and the broken windshield but the deer legs kick hard and quick, snapping back my thumb and forefingers.

I crawl away from my burning vehicle, hands and knees crackling on the dry yellow and orange leaves. I separate. I crack into burning stones. The legs of the buried deer thrash as flames pour outward from my Mom's car through Brains and Tiffany's mouths all the way to skeleton class.

I crawl for hours. My bent-backward fingers throb.

Finally, there's a garage up ahead.

It's Uncle Nick's.

And that was the greatest advantage of living with family: we could help each other in case of an emergency.

Uncle Nick pulls the plastic sheets off his skeleton glass motorcycle and blows away the cobwebs. He has acquired a hunchback over the years. Icicles glint from within his long gray beard.

"You should've paid attention in skeleton class."

He pats the seat of his skeleton glass motorcycle behind him. The glass has a purplish hue that creates light ripples when touched, revealing the skeletal shapes of Tiffany and Brains. I dug them up many times to remove the decaying flesh. Did you ever know bones become soft if chiseled, bleached, cared for, and loved?

I rest my cheek on Uncle Nick's bare shoulder and we roar off into the snowstorm on his skeleton glass motorcycle.

He grins. "I know the way."

We take a right at the top of the plot's driveway down a steep hill resembling a luge course.

As we glide on skeleton glass to skeleton class, the yetis wave to us while watering their lawns covered in snow petunias and snow marigolds with hoses spurting sparkling purple and black ice. I pretend it's skeleton glass because it makes my eyes cold enough to sleep.

Bionica Deseria

Though the bell ring-a-dinged when I entered Jezzelle's Delicacy, Jezzelle kept her back to me as she crushed or choked something discreetly beneath her flour-stained apron.

Crunch.

I drummed my fingers on the register, awaiting my slice of cheesecake.

Hung high on the wall like a bizarre trophy and illuminated by a mini accent spotlight was an ivory-handled horsewhip tipped with a spiked silver ferule. That hadn't been there before.

Jezzelle turned around but, horror of all horrors, she was dressed a bit peculiarly--differently than her back attired in black dress pants and a white chenille sweater (with uncut sale tag). Jutting from her ribs this steel contraption resembled a warrior's chest stabbed by swords and an alien spaceship's glowing control panel; beneath, a laced bodice forced a proffering of her milk and rose petal breasts.

Obscuring most of her face was a cobra mask made of shellacked snakeskin, frayed wood, splintered rope, and rodent fingernails. Revolving emerald eyes interrogated me while her jaw protruded wires, bolts, and poles like something an insane orthodontist would've constructed during a blackout. I tried to scream.

"It looked far more strange and menacing in the daylight than at night in the woods when she slept-walked through the swamp. Her silk nightgown billowed in the wind, slapping flesh to skin, as all the thorny frogs and I faded to red maple," Daniel Trenchwater said as if to no one. He sat alone at a nearby table eating a flan.

She bit through the reptilian alien organ serving as a gag, gushing its translucent juices down her chin. Her eyes were bloodshot and glaring, like a cornered and starving animal.

"Happy Halloween," Jezzelle said, her monstrous snake tongue slapping against her knees. Her smile dropped as she noted my expression. "What will it be?"

"A slice of cheesecake," I said.

Her calendar's pages lifted from the wall as another customer entered, revealing koala bears playing in various seasonal scenes. October's picture featured two koala bears brushing each other's fur with human finger bones in a pile of orange and yellow leaves beside a decaying wooden rake. One of the koala bears looked at me with green swirling fires in his eyes as his nose bled.

Daniel Trenchwater looked up from his flan as Jezzelle slapped the wooden counter; it flipped over, the black marble of its opposite side lined with ten koala bear heads, their eyes scratched out.

She tore open a koala bear head with her bare hands. It burst open, the fluids dribbling down her firm stomach to between her creamy thighs. Licking the lips of her labia, exposed through her shredded canvas shorts, she squirmed and giggled.

"Take a shot with me, loverboy," Jezzelle said as she alternately sucked watermelon-colored brain tissue from the koala bear's skull and continued to pleasure herself. Unblinking, she stared at me as her fiery breath lit up fissures in the magenta smoke surrounding us like lightning in storm clouds. We kissed the deepest kiss I've ever been given, a watermelon jelly dribbling out the sides of our mouths as I squeezed milk from the stiff, upward-pointing tips of her lipstick-painted nipples.

"Ouch," she said.

"Admit it. You love it."

"Come over here, honey bear," she said as a koala bear crawled from beneath her throne wearing Daniel's corduroy coat and black spectacles. He offered his paw by way of introduction. When I lifted my hand, it was a koala bear's paw as well.

I settled onto a stool at the counter and kept swiveling a little so that I'd make eye contact with Daniel Trenchwater as he returned to his seat as a koala bear. But every time I spun, our koala-bear eyes failed to lock. He was again intensely focused on eating that flan of his, in which he'd barely managed to make a dent, despite his unwavering focus on that very task. Then he began to itch at his skin, eventually ripping it and causing a thin tear down the center of his entire koala body as if he'd confused his gray and white fur with a costume. I had to look away as gore fell from the split in his face to his flan.

"Where've you been? Did you disconnect your phone again?" Jezzelle asked, her cobra tongue swinging dangerously close to brushing the top of my cheesecake.

"I'm sorry," I said. "It's been a rotten month."

"You're not still feeling guilty about my nightgown, right? Forget it. We were all so drunk. You both took Polaroids of me naked. Remember that? Made me lift the nightgown and slap it, but I wanted to," Jezzelle said. "I get off when people watch me do it."

She drummed her red fingernails against the marble counter and took another swig from the koala bear's skull.

"I've been fucked up by that night. Daniel cumming in my ear. Calling me his little earwig. Ruining your silk nightgown. Since then? Nothing, really. I just picked up this 60's Italian motorcycle at a garage sale the other day. Wanna go for a ride after work?"

Despite that she wore the eerie cobra mask, I sensed she was blushing.

"Okay," she said, "I close at three, but I probably won't be done cleaning up until four. How does that sound?"

"You'll have to ditch the costume. I don't want that thing digging into my back."

"You can't tell Daniel. He took me to his house again

last night. We got lost on a snowy road. We were following my sister. Our wheel got mangled by a stump. We got out to investigate and then we saw him sleeping there. His drugged, eerie smile. His skin sour candy apple colored."

She chuckled at this and then returned to doing inventory. I went back to work on my cheesecake, disturbed by her admission that she'd been back to Daniel's house.

It was only two o'clock. I considered my options for killing time between then and our ride at four. I decided on the arcade. It was also in Paradise Plaza and the owner (Jamie) had told me last week he was getting a new game (Drowned Machine Souls) that would 'blow my mind.'

I swallowed the last forkful of cheesecake and left a handsome tip Jezzelle would be sure to tease me about later.

"I'll see ya in a bit," I said.

"Seeya, hon," she said a tad flirtatiously.

On my way out, I passed Daniel Trenchwater's table. He eyed the flan as if it held the secret to the greatest enigma in the world--happiness, perhaps.

"Time's a-wasting, buddy," I said, brimming with self-confidence.

His eyes looked fragile behind his magnifying spectacles.

"Stay away from Jezzelle," he said, winking and giving me that look like he wanted me to remember my lips mashed into the wiry hairs of his crotch as beads of sweat rolled out of his fat folds as his stomach rolled in pleasure.

He continued to construct a near microscopic forest of broccoli underneath his plate with his koala paws. His intense concentration hadn't been focused on his flan at all. His eyes shifted from blue to red and a warm numbness filled my lower back.

***

I had parked my bike next to a dumpster in the corner of Jezzelle's parking lot so nobody would mess with it, but I saw a garbage truck shaking a dumpster midair in its forklift-like claws way too close to Isabella: my candy-apple red 175cc CSS Super Sport 'Disco Volante' 1955 Italian motorcycle.

I tried to wave the driver down to stop him from putting my bike in such danger, but he was either drunk or ignoring me. He continued even after I'd hopped on Isabella, started her, and began revving her engine in order to emphasize my point. Being koala bears made it difficult for either of us to operate our machinery, yet by crawling about and swinging from levers, throttles, and pedals, we managed.

"Mmm. You make me purr. Now save me. Cut me. Make me bleed. Drink my rust until dawn," Isabella whispered in between her revving sounds.

As the koala bear driver dropped the dumpster only a few feet away from Isabella, he finally noticed us.

"That your bike?" he asked as he leaned out the passenger-side window, his koala paw patting the back of his side mirror.

"Yeah," I said.

"She for sale?" he asked.

"Nope," I said.

"A beaut, a real beaut," he said as he backed up his truck with that high-pitched beeping sound piercing my ears.

I turned off Isabella and parked her.

"Why not put a little gas in my gasket," Isabella's voice echoed in the silence, "it's about time you spunked in the chamber of the one you love best."

A moment later, I stood high on a bank with grass beneath me and trees on either side, staring down at a raccoon stumbling about and drunkenly hissing as it circled my cherry-red Isabella.

I did not move. The sight of the sick animal transfixed me. He stumbled in a daze, vomiting an orange chunky liquid intermittently. He clawed at the wheel on the back of the dumpster and then sneezed. It was a wheel, not a tire, and it was therefore nothing he could sink his teeth into. He then stumbled over to my bike, my precious Isabella. I had even ordered a black bomber jacket with red leather piping, also vintage, that was identical to the one my favorite proto-punk band's lead singer wore: Rob Younger of Radio Birdman. I fingered the zipper of my beloved jacket, so crisp and so blindingly silver, yet draped over me like a kid in Dracula's cape because of my koala bear body.

The raccoon nestled his teeth into Isabella's front tire, causing a delicate hiss.

"Hey!" I shouted.

He turned to me a little cockeyed and chuckled.

"T-T-T-T-T-T-Tommy! T-t-t-t-t-tell me when it's gone. I w-w-w-w-was attacked by one of them as a kid," the raccoon said. "It's me. Daniel."

I saw the bloody gray and white fur and Mickey Mouse ears of a koala bear beside him on the pavement.

I chucked a rock at him and watched in terror as the path of its arc sent it straight into one of Isabella's side mirrors, shattering it.

There would be no ride with Jezzelle.

I burst at him, wielding a stick and a few stones. I unloaded them, all but one hitting him in the head and torso, except a stray stone that nastily skimmed the body of Isabella, tearing a thin gash into her cherry red paint job. I pinned him down, ready to stomp on him.

"T-T-T-T-T-T-Tommy, please help me," the raccoon Daniel said, shielding his eyes with a bloody claw.

I thought of all the pain and humiliation Daniel

Trenchwater had caused Jezzelle and I during the last month.

I dug the crux of each of the three-prongs of the branch into Daniel the raccoon's neck, but they started snapping. Soon enough, I was just sticking a single, spear-like stick directly into his torso and, on top of everything else, he was ticklish. Trying to spear him though I was, the stick proved too limber and kept bending each time I drove it in for the kill.

I picked Daniel the raccoon up by his tail. As he swung this way and that with his extended claws and vicious teeth, I flung him into the only trap and holding place that proved available: the dumpster.

Daniel screamed. Then he must've fainted, for I heard a loud clunk echo in the bottom of the dumpster like the bass drum Radio Birdman thumped in quick succession at the beginning of their concerts.

Sweat rolled down my forehead as I struggled to catch my breath.

Jamie, who owned and ran the arcade just fifty yards away, had a gun in his filing cabinet.

***

I found Jamie asleep in his office. I tried to rouse him but he must've passed out from another damn binge. I grabbed a half-full cup of coffee and doused him with it. Startled and annoyed, he sat up, his koala bear ears bristling in anger.

"Tommy! What the hell are you doing?" he snarled.

"Quick! Bring your gun!" I said.

***

As we neared the bank that separated the parking lot of his arcade from the parking lot of Jezzelle's Delicacies, he crawled with his shotgun like he was engaged in warfare. Only after he'd reached the top of the bank did he turn to me and say, "Where and what is it?"

"It's Daniel Trenchwater," I said. "He's lost his mind! He ripped off his koala skin and now he's a raccoon."

Jamie got up and brushed the dirt off himself.

"Does that dickwad even realize he's fucking with The Koala Dimension?"

Jamie nodded at me grimly, but then the lid of the dumpster opened and the head of a cobra burst into view.

The tentacle-like robotic arms shook and gyrated as a tower of flame burst from the cobra's head.

Like the intestine, heart, and spleen of a reptile, dark pink and purple organs pulsed and spat syrupy strands that sizzled against our koala bear cheeks.

I've blamed it on Halloween, on the failure of my slow-motion lunge and exclaimed "No!" to cease his fire, and even on Jezzelle herself for wearing such a hideous costume in the first place, but, in the end, all the blame always seemed to fall square back on me for the head shot that Jezzelle then incurred from the shotgun of one Jamie Kellsington.

Her slashed cobra face fell in shreds of blubber to the pavement as I rammed into Jamie while bounding to the dumpster.

As I approached, the raccoon Daniel leapt out.

Another shot then fired.

"What have we done?" I said.

Jamie ran back to his arcade.

A few minutes later, I heard another gunshot. That was the sound of the bullet entering the head of one Jamie Kellsington, as the unshaven officer with the crystal stud earring pointed out later that Halloween evening.

I was mixed up, filled with a childish psychological pain, misunderstood by friends, the papers, the law, and love. I didn't want to hurt anybody but an infinite distance came between me and my date with Jezzelle that afternoon. I felt betrayed, unwound, yet not well-oiled and as though at any moment my jaw might fall from my face, unloosening the coils and springs and the android jaws, I destroyed my face implanting in order to bring back Jezzelle whenever I stare alone and forlorn through my mirror and back to The Koala Dimension. Jezzelle and Jamie both left me their places of business.

I am making a spider web of wire that will one day stretch from Jezzelle's Delicacies to Jamie's Netherworld Nights arcade, a plank that one day might be ready for me to walk and re-walk that fateful path of killed time.

Dorothy Lamour

"Lana, do you remember Dorothy?"

"I remember nothing. I remember everything."

Lana Huntington opened the curtains as she did every morning, but something went terribly wrong: within the television screen it showed Hedy, not Dorothy. Lana started to smash it and bring back her beloved cassette tape toys.

Besides, my eyeliner never looked quite severe enough during those weeks when I'd have Some Girls Wander by Mistake (bald, the green-skinned mouse) or Heaven is Waiting on repeat.

I have to light and smoke another few hand-rolled cigarettes to make the red moths drift away. But most of these pages have already been burnt or washed down the river with the blood and driftwood of all my feathers. I paid a visit to Lana because I wore my prom dress every Halloween morning to evening.

Lana Huntington put on the sparkling-green-in-emeralds tiara. And all the diamond-encrusted insects went flat, their tiny legs twitching.

Although she'd been shocked by an electric fence as a child while slipping down the grassy wet bank in Vermont towards the cow pasture, it was the sight of Lamarr blood-moon-eclipsing Lamour in a Persona-esque crossfade that produced the truly blood-boiling shock now—and which left Lana lingering there, still-pausing the image with a familiar fascination, creeping all-too-readily backwards, retreating, in these few distant years, and reminding her of the dilemma: would she ever speak to Dorothy Lamour? To be to her a second Dorothy Lamour for the length of one solitary exhaled breath? Black pang oil the kiss of spider rockets, says her thighs to her thighs.

There was a wooden casket in the secret room upstairs. Lana Huntington paced back and forth in the kitchen because of what she'd seen through the secret room's window while standing on her lawn: a diamond-studded tiara dripping with long strands of liquefied emerald hovering above the head of a head of a large and ghostly praying-mantis-like insect.

The kid at Permafrost later that evening had looked like a young Bela Lugosi. Three dirty martinis with huge green olives later and his strawberry-gum scent made the air thick as Dolores Delrium lit her mighty flares.

Later: "I'm so sorry. I should have told you…"

Then the phone calls had started again. Lipstick on the telephone's mouthpiece. Hot nights thrashing on the kitchen floor, begging to bite oneself the collapsed and inching finger a riptide 'gainst knife hunger. Lick me through a thousand candy prisons to be electrosexorcuted of me.

Dorothy Lamour was the silent one ceasing to exist. She pretended she couldn't answer it anymore. But she could walk outside of the television at any moment, the white bed-sheet tied around her neck and billowing as she cut her throat in front of all her neighbors.

Lana paused the film on a different image now: Dorothy Lamour, head thrown back in laughter while riding and smoking in the back of a cab driven by a white-cockroach covered Hedy Lamarr. Then another tape, another image. Watching herself naked on her television alone in a white room beside the decapitated and naked bodies of Lamarr and Lamour, Lana Huntington poured herself a strong gin and tonic and began playing with the ice cubes. One golden memory kept recurring: silver thorns, glittering fingernails, and antennae sprouting through twinkling diamonds and the off-white, semi-transparent cockroaches that crawled all over her face and glittered in the darkness—and the unblinking red light of the camera still recording.

The disco ball circled beside slow cigarette smoke clouds. Jets of cold water from the sprinklers pouring down the dress against her knees. The March Violets and The Danse Society usually spun shimmers of elegant Goth decadence most frequently on the turntable at Permafrost that spring.

"I'm not gonna to make love to you. Tonight, I'm gonna fuck you," permafrost as the white frosty hair club kid (young Bela Lugosi) said while turning "A Forest" up to full volume.

Later: would you cringe at the liberally applied Vaseline when the cougar crossed the shadows and grew hungry for the second darker course, too?

Crossfade. The room rocked back and forth. The grayness of the furniture and the light grew dimmer as the lamps flickered and burnt out. Neighbors' dogs had begun a redundant conversation in the darkness as she felt their tiny legs and alert antennae once again envelop her soft skin in a shimmering mask.

"I have always hated Dorothy Lamour."

"It's what you used to do when you couldn't sleep…burn the pictures of the models or actresses or famous musicians. You imagined them at some party in a mansion in Beverly Hills, and all of them were burning."

Lana sat on the couch and flipped on the television. She surfed the channels for awhile (she had cable) and finally decided to watch an old movie starring Dorothy Lamour and Hedy Lamarr (and had an immediate craving for their tyrannously-thirty-thurst-oil-devlish-hot-oil-burning-cross-while-dressed-as-nuns-display-lick-absorb-flesh-curtain-window-to-hollow-apple-core-extract-the-jam-to-feel-my-heart-enfolded-unto-roses river raft scene in Gustav Machatý's Ecstasy), but somebody had already cut out the paper dolls of Lamarrs, replacing them with Lamours as Lana's games could include Red Lorry, Yellow Lorry trying to cover "Bela Lugosi's Dead" in all the little glinting reams of cassette tape fury.

The phone in the kitchen rang three times. Lana decided

to pick it up. She didn't say hello or anything.

"Mrs. Turner?" the voice asked on the other end.

"Execute him," the High Priestess cried, throwing the head of her savagely killed beast slave over her shoulder and cackling as she disappeared on her bionic crystallized dragon into an infinite sand storm.

"Yes," Lana replied even though it was obviously a wrong number.

"You're in serious trouble. I'm watching him scale the side of your house through my binoculars. You must leave there!" the woman finished, hanging up.

"Now look what you've done!" screamed the High Priestess.

Lana returned to the couch to continue watching the film starring Lamour and Lamarr, wishing for the wire-strangulation scene worse than your horniest, mind-altering/rearranging itch ever. At this point in the film, Dorothy's character was caught in a rainstorm out at sea in a sailboat beside Lamarr's decapitated and naked body—as Lamour struggled desperately to undo the sail, Lana still paused the image as a magnifying glass revealed a unique triangle of moles below the downy-haired pubis bone.

There was a knock at the door.

She decided to ignore it but the knocking continued.

It was incredibly windy and pouring outside. The real storm had simply blended in with the storm in the television.

"Hey," said the black and white flickering image of Dorothy Lamour, "do you want to play a video in the game with me?"

Lana got that creepy, closed-in feeling once again like her thoughts were about to sprint away. There's thumbprints all over Dorothy's face, so it's difficult to see this part in the film. But, as portraits go, thumbprints can make the experience so much more intimate and prove you've been there…even when all the white cockroaches rush to commence the formation of the mask.

There stood a teenage girl in a blue and white sports uniform—soccer was her guess—whose slightly-curly hair, all tied up in one big ponytail to the left, was soaking wet. One of her fakeeyelash-surrounded green olive eyes under thin, finely-plucked eyebrows was lazy. She stood still and expectant but shivering…as if posing for photo. Her small but pert and alertly-focused blue lips housed white American teeth, all in perfect squares. Her breastbone etched in relief and shadow-cast by her prominent shoulder bones.

As the girl toyed anxiously (cassette tapes coiling) with her long brown curls, Dorothy Lamour giggled from within the television screen, stroking the blonde hair of Hedy Lamarr's decapitated head (enswarmed in cycles by white cockroaches when the nectar of the cackling moon dripped bright) with a glittering, ivory-handled hairbrush.

Balled up into a fist, Lana's reddening fingers and long red nails dug into her thigh, ripping off flakes of skin and drawing blood. Girls have red eyes. As they wander and drag hot nests by mistake. Leaving trails of honey for our eager/greedy caterpillar eyes.

Dorothy Lamour's character struggled with ropes woven and tangled into the sail (shaped like a butterfly wing) of the boat. Abrasions and tiny cuts defaced her wrists and ankles. Lana grew worried for Dorothy tied to the mast, crucified sideways, stripped through crying head banging agony through the torrential storm. Believe in butterfly wings!

But the High Priestess felt no pity for her slaves!

Lana went upstairs and collected a quilt, a sweatshirt, and a pair of sweatpants. She passed the mirror above her dresser and paused there for a moment: she was surprised to find herself looking more frantic than she felt—her penis was also much smaller and more wrinkled than she recalled;

her face was pinched into a wince, folding over and into itself as if wishing to duplicate Lamour/Lamarr faces.

When Lana returned back downstairs, she found the girl leaning forward, one eye twitching while the other rolled back. Lazy-eyed like Dorothy's?

"Run!" The High Priestess wailed, slashing into the backs of slaves with a tethered whip as sweat and syrupy strands of saliva dripped down her leather girdle.

Then, without a shred of modesty, the girl removed her blue and white soccer uniform and stood there naked as she dried herself off, treating Lana's grandmother's quilt like a towel. But how had she…escaped the bonds…and without any welts or bruises?

Trickling down into the basement, the green liquid emerald sought to form itself into a tiara. The High Priestess had demanded a human sacrifice and Lana knew she had no choice but to comply.

The girl smiled in delight as Lana finally placed the green flaming tiara above her head.

"Please, let Dorothy see!" the girl pleaded.

But the High Priestess screamed. She demanded the blood of the High Ogre Ha'Fiah Toth. It was a fine view: tearing apart his breastbone with her golden teeth, her naked and silver-painted Amazonian body heaving from the exertion and rippling from the pleasure and rejuvenation it received. There was fire on her lungs and the Thi'Amskueellen Forest was burning brighter than usual as the diamond at the center of her emerald-encrusted tiara reflected her blood-hunger backward in a ghostly spiral.

"You can abuse me to your own ends, after a fashion," the slave concurred.

He kneeled before the gold plate with the velvet pouch upon which lay a bone-dry, hand-rolled cigarette containing 38 narcotics from planet Beezelblub Ha'Thwan and a special blend of antioxidants harvested from its fourth moon.

"Enjoy your offering. It shall be thou's final flaeken," The High Priestess urged.

Lana had hardly been paying attention to the picture: Dorothy Lamour was in a bedroom now. As Dorothy Lamour sat on the edge of the bed and smoked, the sewn-off, bloody legs of Lamarr lay on the bed beside her. And why shouldn't a girl like to be playing paper dolls!

Lana asked the girl what happened.

There was a loud knock at the bedroom door in the film.

"Who's there?" Dorothy Lamour said.

"Aren't you going to answer that?" the girl asked Lana.

Lana's front door blew open and the girl shrieked. Lana rushed to close it, but the girl's scream had caused her to lose control of her bladder. She stood near the door as her piss-soaked panties darkened the front of her jean skirt.

The girl turned to concentrate once again on the picture. Lana realized her bladder had not been completely emptied. With the girl's back turned, she allowed the rest of her pee to dribble down her leg. It excited her. The stinging sensation promised a rash. Her feet felt cold and then she looked down at her white, low-cut socks with pink hearts and violet egg-shells around the ankles, light clear-yellow droplets lingering there and refusing to be absorbed into the tiny strands of threaded cotton.

"I just pissed myself." The girl licked her lower lip lightly. "Don't you smell it?"

The girl looked at her a tad defensively, like a cornered animal.

Lana went into the kitchen, removed her wet panties, and threw them into the sink beside a single dirty dish which bore the remnants of the gray and black skin from the salmon she'd grilled earlier that evening. She put a tiny bit of water on a dish towel—she didn't want a lot of water growing dank in the kitchen sink; then she wiped herself, gasping from the chill of it.

Lana cut a mango in two and pressed one half against herself, under her skirt, and squeezed a few slowly-traveling drops of piss into it.

She handed the girl the soiled mango half.

"I want to believe you, sugar. You're not as nuts as they say. Never were," Dorothy Lamour stated demurely as her long green snake tongue slithered about wildly and Lana fell into her growing-to-ladder-length arms, at long last.

Nicholaus Patnaude

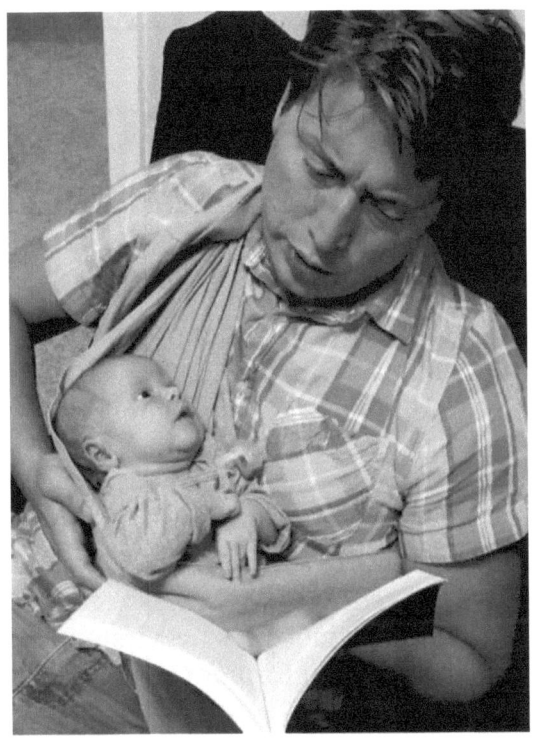

Nicholaus Patnaude grew up in the haunted woods of Connecticut. His illustrated novel, *First Aide Medicine,* was published by Emergency Press. He is editor-in-chief at Psychedelic Horror Press. He lives with his wife and son near Shenandoah National Park.

The New Bizarro Author Series

2009-2010
Carnageland by D.W. Barbee
Naked Metamorphosis by Eric Mays
Sex Dungeon for Sale by Patrick Wensink
Rotten Little Animals by Kevin Shamel

2010-2011
How to Eat Fried Furries by Nicole Cushing
Muscle Memory by Steve Lowe
Felix and the Sacred Thor by James Steele
Love in the Time of Dinosaurs by Kirsten Alene
Uncle Sam's Carnival of Copulating Inanimals
    by Kirk Jones
The Egg Said Nothing by Caris O'Malley
Bucket of Face by Eric Hendrixson

2011-2012
A Hollow Cube is a Lonely Space by S.D. Foster
Lepers and Mannequins by Eric Beeny
Party Wolves in My Skull by Michael Allen Rose
Seven Seagulls for a Single Nipple
    by Troy Chambers
Gigantic Death Worm by Vince Kramer
The Placenta of Love by Spike Marlowe
Trashland A Go-Go by Constance Ann Fitzgerald
The Crud Masters by Justin Grimbol

2012-2013
Gutmouth by Gabino Iglesias
Avoiding Mortimer by J.W. Wargo

Her Fingers by Tamara Romero
Kitten by G. Arthur Brown
Janitor of Planet Anilingus
    by Andrew Wayne Adams
House Hunter S.T. Cartledge

2013-2014
The Mondo Vixen Massacre by Jamie Grefe
The Cheat Code for God Mode by Andy De Fonseca
Babes in Gangland by Bix Skahill
8-bit Apocalypse by Amanda Billings
Grambo by Dustin Reade
There's No Happy Ending by Tiffany Scandal
The Church of TV as God by Daniel Vlasaty

2014-2015
SuperGhost by Scott Cole
Pax Titanus by Tom Lucas
Deep Blue by Brian Auspice

2015-2016
King Space Void by Anthony Trevino
Rainbows Suck by Madeleine Swann
Arachnophile by Betty Rocksteady
Benjamin by Pedro Proenca
Rock 'n' Roll Head Case by Lee Widener
Slasher Camp for Nerd Dorks by Christoph Paul
Elephant Vice by Chris Meekings
Pixiegate Madoka by Michael Sean Le Sueur
Towers by Karl Fischer

2016-2017
Guitar Wolf by Nicholaus Patnaude
Hate From the Sky by Sean M Thompson
Aunt Post by John Wayne Comunale
Tetraminion by R.A. Roth